Dⁱˢⁿᵉᵖ · PIXAR

FINDING NEMO

DON'T INVITE
A SHARK TO DINNER
AND OTHER LESSONS FROM THE SEA

D1309650

A STEPPING STONE BOOK™

Random House 🏠 New York

Library of Congress Control Number: 2002113525

ISBN: 0-7364-2125-4

Printed in the United States of America

10 9 8 7 6 5 4 3 2 1

www.randomhouse.com/kids/disney

DISNEP · PIXAR
FINDING
NEMO

DON'T INVITE A SHARK TO DINNER
AND OTHER LESSONS FROM THE SEA

BY MARLIN A. CLOWNFISH
as told to Kiki Thorpe
With special help from
Jasmine Jones

Designed by Disney's Global Design Group

INTRODUCTION

Life can be tough for a little fish. As if paddling around all day with tiny fins wasn't enough to keep you busy, you constantly have to keep an eye out for predators. One thing I've learned is that anything that *can* eat you *will*. So if you're a pint-sized swimmer like me, even one lap around the coral can be hazardous to your health. It can make the ocean seem pretty scary.

Believe me, I know. I used to be a scaredy-fish. I never left the safety of my anemone home if I could help it. I was even afraid of sea slugs! But then one day my son, Nemo, was taken away by a scuba diver. I had to travel hundreds of miles through the open water to find him. It was a journey that changed my life.

Ever since then, fish have been asking me, "Marlin, how did a little clownfish like you survive out there in the ocean?" I tell them it wasn't easy. It took a lot of luck—and a lot of help from my friends. When it was over, I realized that life's too short to spend it hiding in a shell. (No offense to you hermit crabs out there.) Sometimes you have to look your fears right in their big, scary mouths. You might find that they aren't really scary after all.

So before you go exploring in the great blue sea, make sure to read this survival guide—and everything should go swimmingly.

CHAPTER 1
LIFE ON THE REEF
A FEW TIPS FOR BEGINNERS

TIP #1 DRESS FOR SUCCESS

Lionfish, tiger sharks, and barracudas—oh, my! There are dangers lurking around every corner on the reef. If you're going out alone, or even with friends, try not to stand out. The last thing you want is to look like a tourist.

I recommend wearing something that blends in with your surroundings. Personally, I prefer bright orange and white stripes, but blues, yellows, and even purples go nicely with the local corals. Stay away from plaids and polka dots. Try for a natural look.

Keep in mind that being extremely colorful is an advantage only on the reef. Out in the open water, a few neon stripes on your tail might as well be a sign that says **FREE LUNCH**! But when you're cruising in the coral, you'll be almost invisible. Remember, if they can't see you, they can't eat you!

DO

DON'T

◀TIP #2▶ LOOK SHARP

If orange coral and bright orange stripes aren't your style, don't worry. There are other ways to get rid of unwanted predators. A set of sharp, prickly spines sends a real "look but don't touch" message. Sea urchins are famous for their spikes. But you don't have to be a bottom-feeder to look sharp. For example, take Nemo's friend Bloat, the blowfish. Whenever he gets scared, he puffs out his sides and ... *poof!* He turns into a floating pincushion! Now, that's a fish that's hard to swallow!

SHAKE A FIN . . .

. . . or a limb! If a big fish gets hold of one of your limbs, let him have it! I know several starfish who use this trick. They say it works great, because starfish can grow back their arms. After all, it's better to lose your arm than to lose your head.

WARNING: Only give up a limb if you know you can grow another. Please check with your doctor if you're not sure.

TIP #4 LOCATION, LOCATION, LOCATION

When choosing your home on the reef, think carefully. Will you live on the flat part of the reef? Or will you live on the reef crest, where the waves break overhead? Maybe you'll choose the reef front, the steep part of the reef that drops into deeper water. A lot of fish will try to sell you reef-front property. Sure, you'll have great views of the ocean. But think about it: Do you really want to be the first thing a shark sees when he drops by for a snack?

TIP #5 KNOW YOUR ENEMY

Or at least know a little bit about him. It can come in handy when you least expect it.

One day I was swimming around the reef, minding my own business, when I bumped into a strange purple-spotted rock. Imagine my surprise when the rock opened its mouth and snarled at me. It wasn't a rock at all—it was a moray eel!

I was out of there in a flash. But the moray eel was right behind me. I tried every trick I could think of to shake him. I darted through a sea fan and doubled back through some thorny coral. But no matter what I did, that eel slithered right after me. I could feel his jaws snapping just inches away from my tail!

Suddenly I remembered that moray eels hunt by smell, not by sight. So if I could find a way to plug the eel's nose, he wouldn't be able to track me down.

Quick as a wink, I dove down to the ocean floor. As the eel came up behind me, I swished my tail in the sand. Sand flew into the eel's face and up his nose. When he stopped to shake himself off, I darted into some thick seaweed.

I hid in the seaweed and held very still. A second later, the eel slithered right past. He couldn't smell me at all. My trick had worked!

Since then, I've been studying up on all the predators on the reef. Did you know that reef sharks have really good hearing? And the stonefish has a row of spines on its back filled with deadly poison. (Now, that's one rock you don't want to add to your collection.)

Do some research on the big fish that hunt in your own neighborhood. Take it from me—a little knowledge goes a long way.

REMEMBER THE FOOD CHAIN

I'll admit it. Clownfish aren't that high on the food chain. Don't get me wrong; I'm no bottom-feeder. But I know there are a whole lot of fish out there who could eat me. It's enough to make a guy feel a little insecure.

The important thing to remember about the food chain is that it's a *chain*. No matter who is trying to eat you, someone else is probably trying to eat *him*. Believe it or not, there are times when the best thing you can do is head straight for a shark—like when a huge tuna is hot on your tail! The tuna will forget about you and swim for the hills. *Voilà!* You're free.

FISH FOOD

If it's a shark you're trying to shake, find a dolphin. Dolphins hate sharks. They use their pointed noses to ram the shark's soft underbellies. Ouch! That would make anyone lose his appetite.

So even if you're as mini as a minnow or as slow as a sea snail, don't be discouraged. If you know how the food chain works, you can make it work for you.

ANEMONE EVACUATION PROCEDURE

I call this technique PESOBIRRRRRRPOG. (Okay, so the name doesn't make much sense. You try coming up with a catchy name for something that has twelve steps.)

I am a bit too advanced for this technique after my journey across the ocean, but beginners, take heed.

STEP 1

PEEK

The first thing to do is look out of the anemone. Don't *go* out—just look. Anything with enormous teeth out there? No? Good. But you still have to be careful. You never know when something is lurking behind a patch of seaweed. Does any of the seaweed look suspicious? No? What about that piece—isn't it a little *extra green*? Better keep an eye on that one.

STEP 2 — EASY DOES IT

Now, ease your nose out of the anemone. Ease it out . . . just a little. Wait! Stop! I said just your nose! *Whew!*

STEP 3 — SWIM OUT AND BACK IN

Next, swim out a little bit, then swim right back into the anemone. That's right—if there's anyone out there, they'll see you and come straight for you. Let them get a mouthful of stinging anemone. Say it with me— swim ooooout, then back.

STEP 4

REPEAT

Swim ooooout, then back.

STEPS 5-9

REPEAT, REPEAT, REPEAT, REPEAT, REPEAT

Swim ooooout, then back. Swim ooooout, then back. Swim ooooout, then back. Swim ooooout, then back. Swim ooooout, then back. Okay, that's enough. Unless you want to do a few more. Whatever you're comfortable with.

STEP 10

PECTORAL FIN OUT

Okay, now swim to the edge of the anemone and stick out your pectoral fin. Wave it around like a flag. That's right— wiggle it. If razor-toothed fish are waiting for you to come out, they'll think you're insulting them. Let me tell you, the fin wiggle makes them mad. Just be ready to slip right back into the anemone if they come near you.

STEP 11
OVERHEAD CHECK

Next, you've got to look up. Many fish get so distracted looking out for what's in *front* of them, they forget to see if anyone is swimming *over* them. Any claws or jaws? If the answer is anything but no, stay where you are.

STEP 12
GO FOR IT!

Okay, now you're ready to swim out of the anemone. But swim quickly. Faster! *Faster!* Don't get caught! Hide behind some coral if you have to!

CHAPTER 2
BEWARE THE BOAT
DIVERS CAN BE DANGEROUS

Barracudas and moray eels are scary, all right. But one of the most terrifying things you'll see around the reef isn't a fish—it's a boat. Very little is known about boats, but they are easy to identify. They have huge round bellies and are almost always found floating on the surface.
Do not confuse a boat with a sleeping manatee or walrus. Boats are not nearly as friendly, although their breath may be better.

If you come across a boat when you're swimming, exercise extreme caution. A diver may be nearby. Divers, also known as humans, may look harmless. But they can be very dangerous creatures. My son, Nemo, was captured by a diver and kept for a while in a fish tank in Sydney. I have also heard of divers who try to collect shells *while their owners are still living in them*! Even sharks are afraid of divers. (Although I have met a few sharks who say they are tasty.)

Unlike fish, divers emit a stream of bubbles wherever they go. This is a sign that they are very gaseous creatures. Use caution when breathing around a diver.

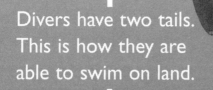

Divers have two tails. This is how they are able to swim on land.

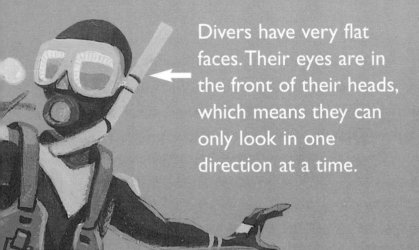

Divers have very flat faces. Their eyes are in the front of their heads, which means they can only look in one direction at a time.

Instead of side fins, divers have pinchers. They use these pinchers for grabbing. Unlike a crab's claws, divers' pinchers are soft and tender. If a diver grabs you, nibble his pinchers. He will quickly retreat. Divers hate nibbling.

Fortunately, divers are extremely clumsy swimmers. Even a clam can swim better than a diver. Divers are also attracted to bright colors. And, for reasons we don't understand, they like to pick up starfish. If a diver is after you, swim quickly and warn any brightly colored starfish so they can run ... er ... so they know they're about to be picked up.

Divers are not the only danger around boats. Some boats have nets, which they use to scoop up entire schools of fish! Fishing boats are usually found within a few miles of land. But stay on the lookout! They have also been spotted far out at sea.

Not far from Sydney, my friend Dory was caught in a fishing net along with a whole school of groupers. Nemo had an idea to help them escape. He was going to swim into the net and tell all the fish to swim downward. He told me to swim around the outside to tell the other fish. I was afraid to let him go in. I had already lost Nemo once, when the diver kidnapped him. I wasn't about to lose him again. But I had to help Dory!

Then I looked at Nemo. He had a brave smile on his little orange face. "Dad, I can do this!" he cried.

"You're right," I agreed. "I know you can!" We slapped fins; then he started to swim.

I swam down to the bottom of the net. "Everybody listen!" I yelled to all the groupers. "Swim down! Don't give up—keep swimming!" I could hear Nemo inside that huge pile of fish, shouting, "Swim down! Swim down!" Dory was shouting, too. "Just keep swimming! Just keep swimming!"

Pretty soon, the groupers caught on. They all began to swim away from the boat. As the net moved up, up, up toward the surface, the groupers swam down, down, down toward the ocean floor.

Just as the net reached the surface, it stopped. Then it slowly began to reverse direction. The fish were pulling it right back down into the water! The groupers swam so hard, they pulled the fishing boat over on its side. The net broke open. All the fish spilled out into the water! They were free!

So remember . . . if you get caught in a fishing net, don't panic. Just tell the fish around you, "Keep swimming!" You're all in it together, and you can all get out of it together.

CHAPTER 3
DON'T TRUST
ANYONE WITH 1600 TEETH

Many fish think that sharks are nothing but mindless eating machines. I'd like to set the record straight. Just because sharks have powerful jaws, rows of razor-sharp teeth, and a taste for blood doesn't mean they're all bad guys. In fact, some of my best friends are sharks. On the other hand, just because they're my friends doesn't mean I totally trust them.

I met my first shark out in deep waters. Normally, a bite-sized, neon-striped fellow like me wouldn't be swimming around in the open like that. But I was trying to find the boat that had taken Nemo.

I was swimming in circles until I met a regal blue tang fish named Dory. She'd seen the boat, and told me which way it was heading. I followed her until I realized that she suffers from short-term memory loss. She's so forgetful that she couldn't remember why I was following her. I was about to leave her when I turned around... and found myself face to face with a great white shark!

The shark flashed a smile that sent shivers down my spine. "Hello," he said. "Name's Bruce. How would you morsels like to come to a little get-together I'm having?"

Normally, I would turn down an invitation to any party where I might be the appetizer. But Bruce smiled again, showing his six rows of very sharp teeth. Then he pulled me under his fin and started dragging me away. How could I refuse?

Bruce led Dory and me to an old sunken submarine surrounded by an underwater minefield. As we swam into the sub, I caught a glimpse of the other party guests—a hammerhead and a mako! I nearly fainted! We were done for!

But believe it or not, the sharks didn't want to eat us. They wanted to be our friends! Bruce and the other two sharks, Anchor and Chum, are part of a group that has a very pleasant attitude toward other fish. They are vegetarians. They even have a little speech they recite together. It goes like this:

I am a nice shark,
not a mindless eating machine.
If I am to change this image,
I must first change myself.
Fish are friends, not food.

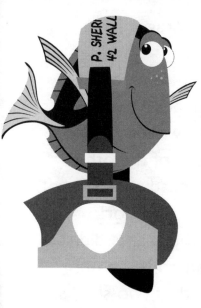

During the party I spotted a diving mask with writing on it. It looked just like the mask on the diver that took my son. I thought it might be a clue to finding Nemo, but I needed someone to read it. Suddenly Dory grabbed the mask. We were far enough away to escape the sharks, but she was going to ask *them* to read it!

When I tried to take it, she held on tight, and the mask snapped back and bonked her in the face. Her nose started to bleed. It was just a trickle, but it was enough.

The instant Bruce smelled blood, it was as if an alarm went off in his brain. He turned from a friendly vegetarian into... well, a mindless eating machine! With a snap of his jaws, he lunged at Dory. If Anchor and Chum hadn't held him back, he would have swallowed us both in one gulp!

WARNING

WHAT TO DO IF YOU SEE A GREAT WHITE SHARK BARRELING TOWARD YOU WITH ITS MOUTH WIDE OPEN

1. Remain calm.
2. Take a deep breath.
3. Swim for your life!

Dory and I raced through the submarine. Bruce had broken free from Anchor and Chum and was right on our tails, snarling and gnashing his teeth like a rabid dogfish. He surged toward us and managed to catch the mask in his teeth. We dodged him and dove into a dark tunnel. But we soon found that there was no way out. The tunnel was blocked . . . by a torpedo!

In his frenzy, Bruce began to slam his nose into the tunnel. *Wham! Wham! Wham!* Behind us, the torpedo was shaking loose. Only a single bolt was holding it in place. It looked as if we were safe for the moment. But Bruce still had the mask in his mouth.

"I need to get that mask!" I told Dory. I was sure it could help me find Nemo.

"Okay!" Dory cried. Before I could stop her, she pushed the bolt out. The torpedo slid out of the launching tube. And we slid with it—right into Bruce's mouth!

Luckily, Bruce's jaws locked on the torpedo. That gave us just enough time to grab the mask and dash back into the safety of the tube.

Furious, Bruce spit out the torpedo. He was just about to dive after us again. But suddenly he realized the torpedo was falling straight toward a live mine! It was about to explode!

The sharks swam away faster than you can say *underwater carnivore*. A second later the mine exploded. *KA-BOOOM!* Fortunately, Dory and I were safe inside the launching tube.

Since then, Bruce, Anchor, and Chum have become my friends. Bruce always apologizes for having tried to eat me. I tell him, "No hard feelings. It could happen to anyone." I think it would be nice if sharks and fish could be friends. The ocean is big enough for all of us, and there's plenty of algae to go around.

However, you never know when a shark's killer instincts could kick in. If you do decide to befriend a shark, there are a few simple precautions you can take to keep "accidents" from happening:

 Try not to look delicious.

 Always provide plenty of snacks. It's unwise to hang out with a hungry shark.

 Avoid getting scrapes, nicks, or cuts of any kind.

 Have a torpedo handy, just in case of emergencies.

CHAPTER 4

DO BE AFRAID

OF THE DARK

A lot of fish have
asked me, "What's the
scariest thing you've seen
in the ocean?" I tell them
that being stared down by a
barracuda can certainly give you the
willies. And getting a close-up look at
a shark's tonsils is no picnic, either. But
scariest of all was the fish I *didn't* see.

Back when I was a young clownfish, we used to sit around the fire coral at night telling scary stories. I remember one about a horrible monster with huge fangs that lived at the bottom of the ocean. It was said to have a magical, glowing light attached to its forehead. It used the light to lure silly little fish to their deaths. I always thought the story was make-believe. Little did I know.

If you've never visited the darkest underwater depths, I have just five words for you: Avoid it at all costs! Some of the weirdest, creepiest creatures in the ocean are swimming around down there. And you can bet you don't want to bump into them.

When Dory and I escaped from the sharks, we ended up on the edge of a deep ocean trench. Down below, there was nothing but cold, black water. Now, I am by nature a tropical fish. I like warm, sunny lagoons. I would never have set fin in that dark abyss if Dory hadn't accidentally dropped the scuba mask. We needed that mask—it was our only clue to finding Nemo! So I took a deep breath and swam down toward the bottom of the ocean.

As we swam deeper and deeper, the water got colder and darker. Finally it was pitch-black. I couldn't see my fin in front of my face. I had no idea how we were going to find the mask.

After a while we saw a tiny bright light up ahead. We swam closer and saw a little glowing ball. It looked so pretty, just floating there in the darkness. Watching it, I felt happier than I had in days. When the ball began to dance around, we giggled and followed it.

Suddenly I had the creepy feeling that we were being watched. Just then we heard something growl right behind us! I turned around . . . and came face to face with the most terrifying thing I have ever seen in my life!

Its mouth was as big as a cavern. Its needle-like fangs were as long as my body. It stared at us with dull, lifeless eyes as it waved a glowing light attached to a long antenna on its forehead. It was a huge, horrible anglerfish. It looked just like the monster from the stories around the fire coral!

Dory and I screamed and took off. Only we didn't know which way we were going. We still couldn't see a thing ... until a dim light lit up the water around us. Unfortunately, it was the anglerfish again!

As I swam away, I looked down and saw the mask on the ocean floor! I grabbed Dory and pulled her down—and just in the nick of time, too! As we ducked, the anglerfish raced over our heads.

"Read the mask!" I told Dory. I couldn't read human, but I knew she could. If she could read the words written on the mask, we might be able to find Nemo!

But it was too dark for Dory to see. I had to get the light back. Dodging this way and that, I lured the anglerfish closer to the mask. Then I ducked for cover behind some rocks. Grabbing the monster's antenna, I held its light toward the mask.

"P. Sherman ....," Dory read.

But before she could go on, the

anglerfish jerked its head back, yanking me away from the rocks. With a snap of its horrible jaws, it swallowed me alive!

Luckily, I was still holding on to the anglerfish's light as I was going in. I guess it didn't like snacking on its own antenna, because a second later it spit me back out. When the light shone on the mask again, Dory read, "42 Wallaby Way."

42 Wallaby Way? That sounded like an address! Now we were getting somewhere. If Dory could only read the last part . . .

By now the anglerfish was furious. With a hideous growl, he barreled toward us through the water.

Just as Dory read the last word—"Sydney!"—I screamed, "Duck!" Dory ducked. I grabbed the mask and held it up like a shield. *Slam!* There was a blinding flash as the anglerfish plowed into me. Then everything went dark. I was sure I was dead.

But when I opened my eyes, I saw that the anglerfish was stuck in the mask. And the mask was wedged between two rocks. He was trapped! The monster thrashed with rage, but he couldn't get us.

Now that we had the address, we didn't need the mask. Before the monster could break free, I grabbed Dory and swam out of there.

That was my first adventure in the deepest, darkest waters of the ocean. And I hope it was my last.

A few nights ago, I was sitting around the fire coral swapping fish tales when someone told a story about *giant squid*. She said these squid are as big as whales, with eyes the size of sea turtles, and tentacles lined with rows and rows of suckers to trap their prey. Supposedly these monsters live in the deepest, darkest part of the ocean, too. Now, this sure sounds like make-believe to me. But I'm not going down there to find out. And I suggest you don't, either.

CHAPTER 5

A FISH

OUT OF WATER

While the ocean depths may be dangerous for a clownfish, things aren't much better at the surface. If you're a fish out of water, you're in a whole peck of trouble—because a whole lot of trouble is going to be pecking at you! Many fish have popped above the surface to have a look around, only to find themselves snatched up by hungry seabirds. Knowing how to avoid seabirds is important for any fish who plans on poking his head out of the water.

Seagulls are some of the most common seabirds. They can be easily identified by their screaming call, which sounds like "Mine! Mine! Mine!" Seagulls are greedy and will eat just about anything. I've heard other birds call them rats with wings. Fortunately, because seagulls aren't that picky, they won't go out of their way to hunt you. They're satisfied with any unlucky fish who happens to get stranded on shore.

If you find yourself beached on a rock or a pier, try to get back in the water as soon as possible. The best way to move quickly across dry surfaces is to employ the *flip-flop* technique (invented by the famous French flounder, Philippe Phlopp). The flip-flop technique has three basic steps:

 **STEP 1** Flail about until you are lying on your side with your tail pointed in the direction you want to go.

STEP 2 Bend your body sideways so that your head and tail lift off the ground.

 **STEP 3** Snap your tail firmly against the ground. The force of this movement should catapult you onto your other side.

Repeat these three steps several times, moving in the direction of a body of water.

If the flip-flop technique does not work for you, there are other means of above-water escape. Dory and I once dodged a flock of hungry seagulls by leaping into the mouth of a friendly pelican. Pelicans have large, bowl-shaped bills that can be filled with water, so we were able to travel quickly through the air in relative comfort and safety. However, this technique is generally not recommended, since most pelicans also eat fish.

If you leap into the mouth of a pelican for safety only to find that the pelican wants to eat you, try this:

1. Twist sideways as you move through the pelican's mouth. Try to get your body lined up across its tongue.

2. When the pelican swallows, wedge yourself in its throat. This will cause the pelican to start coughing.

3. When the pelican coughs you out, use the flip-flop technique (see previous page) to reach the nearest body of water.

Do not stop swimming once you hit the big blue, however. Just because you're below sea level doesn't mean you're safe.

Once I was swimming near the coast when I heard a huge splash in the water next to me. At first I thought it was a flying fish coming in for a crash landing. But suddenly I saw a giant bird shooting through the water! It was a cormorant, and he looked hungry.

I dove straight down, thinking the cormorant wouldn't be able to follow me. But the bird stayed right on my tail, paddling with its webbed feet and using its tail like a rudder. I'm a pretty fast swimmer, but the cormorant was faster. Without thinking, I dove into a crack between two rocks. *Slam!* The bird crashed into the rocks and caught its beak in the crack. I had just enough time to swim away before it yanked its beak free. Lucky for me, cormorants don't have gills, and this big bird had run out of steam. As the cormorant darted back up to the surface for a breath of air, I swam out of there.

Visiting the surface can be an exciting experience. There's a whole world up there that is still relatively unexplored by fishkind. But if you do decide to take the risk, watch out for those so-called fine-feathered friends.

CHAPTER 6
ALWAYS FOLLOW DIRECTIONS
IF YOU CAN REMEMBER THEM

Almost all fish know the rule "Trust your instincts." But there's another rule of ocean survival that's just as important: "Trust your friends." Your pals will look out for you, and they'll let you know if you're taking a wrong turn. I learned this lesson the hard way when Dory and I were trying to find the East Australian Current.

I knew I had to get to Sydney to find Nemo. But I didn't have any idea where Sydney was. Luckily, a group of passing moonfish gave Dory and me directions. They told us to follow the East Australian Current for about three leagues. It would take us right to Sydney.

If you want to travel quickly down the coast of Australia, the EAC is a great way to go. But I was in such a hurry to get there that I took off without waiting for the rest of the directions. The moonfish told Dory, "When you come to this trench, swim *through* it, not over it."

Unfortunately, Dory's memory is not exactly her strongest asset. By the time she caught up with me, she'd forgotten what the moonfish had told her.

Before long, Dory and I came to a deep trench in the ocean floor. The trench was dark and full of strange, echoing sounds. It looked pretty spooky to me. "We're gonna swim over this thing," I said to Dory.

But even though Dory had forgotten most of

the moonfish's instructions, she remembered a part of them. "Something is telling me we should swim *through* it, not over it," she told me.

"Are you even looking at this thing?" I asked. "It's got death written all over it! Over we go."

"Come on," Dory said. "Trust me on this."

But I did not trust Dory. Instead, I tricked her. "Look!" I cried. I pretended to see something in the water ahead of us. "Something shiny!"

"Where?" Dory asked.

"Oh, it just swam over the trench," I told her. "Come on, we'll follow it."

"Okay!" Dory exclaimed. She had already forgotten the small part of the moonfish's warning that she had remembered just moments before, and she followed me through the clear blue water above the trench. Bright sunlight shone down, and we could see everything for miles around. Which was just how I wanted it.

Pretty soon we noticed the East Australian Current up ahead of us, rushing along like an underwater river. "There's the current," I told Dory. "We should be there in no time."

But Dory wasn't listening to me. She was staring at a tiny blob in the water. "Come here, little squishy," Dory said as she reached out to touch it. When her fin brushed against the blob, it stung her!

"Ow!" Dory cried, quickly pulling her fin back.

Just then I realized what the blob was. "Dory, that's a jellyfish!" I cried. Quickly, I pushed the little jellyfish away. The jellyfish stung my fin, too, but it didn't hurt me as much as it hurt Dory. That's because I live in an anemone, which has stinging tentacles a lot like a jellyfish's. The anemone's tentacles don't hurt me because I brush against them every day.

I checked Dory's fin to see if it was okay. The jellyfish sting hurt a lot, but it didn't look too bad. "Let's be thankful it was just a little one," I said.

But I'd spoken too soon! When I looked up, I saw hundreds of jellyfish blocking our path. They had drifted down around us while I was looking at Dory's fin. I turned this way and that, but there was nothing but jellyfish as far as the eye could see. We were trapped!

"Hey! Watch this!" Dory said suddenly. To my horror, she started bouncing up and down on top of a jellyfish!

"Dory, don't bounce on the tops!"
I cried. As I rushed over to stop her,
she bounced away onto another
jellyfish. The tops of the jellyfish weren't
hurting her! Only the jellyfish's tentacles
were poisonous. If we could just get
past them without touching their
tentacles, we'd be safe.

"All right, listen to me. I have an
idea—a game," I told her. "Whoever can
hop the fastest out of these jellyfish
wins. Rules, rules, rules! You can't touch
the tentacles—only the tops."

"Something about tentacles. Got it!"
Dory said. "On your mark, get set, go!"
Before I could stop her, she raced away.

"No, wait! Dory!" I cried.
She hadn't heard what I'd said
about the tentacles! "Wait
a minute! Whoa!" But it
was too late. She was
already far ahead of me.

I bounced on top of the rubbery jellyfish, trying to catch up with her. *Boing! Boing! Boing!* I bounced faster and faster. Oddly enough, I was having fun!

With a mighty bounce, I caught up with Dory. Together we raced through that poisonous pink jungle, laughing our heads off. Suddenly I could see clear blue water up ahead. Only a few more bounces and we'd be away from the jellyfish!

I shot ahead like a bolt of lightning. One last bounce landed me in clear, jellyfish-free water. "The clownfish is the winner!"

But when I turned to Dory, she wasn't there. I looked all around, but she was nowhere in sight. With a sinking feeling, I hurried back to find her. But now more and more jellyfish were descending. I could hardly squeeze through them. It was almost a solid wall of jellyfish!

At last I spotted Dory. She was wrapped up in the tentacles of a jellyfish. Her eyes were closed, and she wasn't moving.

"Dory!" I screamed. I shot into the tentacles and grabbed her. The tentacles burned me, but I managed to pull her out. She was still breathing— but barely.

"Am I disqualified?" she asked weakly.

"No, you're doing fine. You're actually winning," I told her. "But you've got to stay awake."

I started to swim back the way I'd come. But the jellyfish were closing in on us. In another minute, there would be no way out! Just then I spied a patch of blue water off in the distance. Quickly I swam toward the opening. It was our last chance to escape!

But this time, I couldn't bounce. The jellyfish were too close together now, and I was carrying Dory. I had to swim past their tentacles. Ow! Ow! Ow! One after another, the poisonous tentacles brushed against me. My immunity was being overpowered, and I could feel myself growing weaker with each sting.

Just as we reached the exit, a humongous jellyfish floated down and stopped right in front of us. There was no way around it. I would have to swim right though its tentacles. Taking a deep breath, I darted toward them. As the tentacles touched my scales, I felt a burning pain shoot through my body. But I kept on swimming. At last I made it out the other side. Then I lost consciousness.

Fortunately, a sea turtle named Crush and his family picked Dory and me up and carried us to the East Australian Current.

If it hadn't been for those turtles, we might never have made it out of there alive! To this day, Dory still has scars from where the jellyfish stung her. If only I'd trusted her when she said we should swim *through* the trench, she might never had been hurt.

Don't forget that the ocean can be a rough place for a little fish, and you can't always make it alone in the big leagues. Listen to your friends when they have something important to tell you. And always—did you hear me say *always*?—follow directions.

CHAPTER 7

IN THE BELLY

OF THE BEAST

The biggest and loudest creatures you'll ever bump into in the ocean are whales. Blue whales can be as big as 98 feet long and weigh as much as 170 tons! They are *the* biggest creatures on earth—I'm talking land, water, *and* sky. These things are, shall we say, a *bit* intimidating to us smaller and quieter beings.

Lucky for us, blue whales don't eat fish.

Instead, they eat tiny shrimp called krill by straining them through large comblike hairs in their mouths called baleen. Unfortunately, if you're not much bigger than the krill, you could end up as whale food, too.

And that's exactly what happened to Dory and me. We were swimming in some murky water off the coast of Sydney when we stopped to ask a little fish for directions. Suddenly a swarm of screaming krill rushed past us. As it got closer, we realized it wasn't a little fish we were talking to at all. It was a great big whale! And it was ready for dinner!

Dory and I started to swim for our lives, but we didn't stand a chance. As the whale sucked up the krill, we went flying head over tail into the whale's mouth.

The funny thing about getting swallowed by a whale is that it feels a lot like being swept up in an extra-strong current. You may not even realize what has happened! If you think you may have been swallowed by a whale but aren't certain, ask yourself the following questions:

1. WHAT IS THE ATMOSPHERE HERE LIKE?

(a) bright and sunny

(b) dark and gloomy

2. WHAT IS THE WATER AROUND ME LIKE?

(a) fresh and clear

(b) dank and stale

3. WHAT IS THE OCEAN FLOOR MADE UP OF?

(a) rocks and coral

(b) taste buds

If you answered (b) to any of these questions, chances are you have been swallowed by a whale!

It's natural to feel upset. When Dory and I landed in the whale's mouth, I felt angry and frustrated. I would never find Nemo! I swam up to the front of the whale's mouth, looking for a way out, but the whale's baleen held us in like bars on a cage.

"I have to get out! I have to find my son!" I shouted. I pounded against the baleen. But it was no use. The whale didn't seem to hear.

"It's all right. It'll be okay," Dory told me. She had already forgotten that we were stuck inside a whale!

"No, it won't," I told her. "I promised Nemo I'd never let anything happen to him."

"Hmm," Dory said. "That's a funny thing to promise. You can't *never* let anything happen to him. Then nothing would ever happen to him."

That gave me something to think about. Had I been too protective of Nemo? I didn't have much time to wonder, however, because at that moment the water around us began to disappear. It was draining out of the whale's mouth and into its stomach!

Suddenly, without warning, the

whale's tongue leaped up toward the top of its mouth. Dory and I sailed high into the air. We had to hang on to the whale's taste buds to keep from falling. I looked down and saw its huge throat.

Just then we heard the whale moan. Its voice boomed so loudly that I could feel it vibrate in my bones. I didn't understand what it said. But Dory did.

"Okay!" she said. Suddenly she let go of the whale's tongue!

"Dory!" I screamed. I grabbed her fin to keep her from falling.

But Dory had meant to fall. "He says it's time to let go," she told me.

I looked down again at the bottomless pit below us. Letting go didn't seem like such a good idea to me. "How do you know something bad isn't going to happen?" I asked Dory.

"I don't!" Dory cried.

I gulped, took a deep breath . . . and let go of the whale's tongue. Down we tumbled into the whale's throat. We fell for what felt like a mile. I thought I'd never see light again.

After a while we were sucked into a stream of water. We weren't falling down anymore. We were traveling up!

KEY PHRASE IN WHALE

Suddenly, we shot out the top of the whale's head. He had blown us out his blowhole! Seconds later we were swimming in the ocean again. He had taken us to Sydney!

So if you get swallowed by a whale, don't worry. Just remember: Let go!

Hello
Mnnnooooooooaaahh

My name is . . .
Oooooooooaoaoooaooooaooooooagh . . .

Can you tell me how to get to Sydney?
Eeeeeeeeaaaaaaghaaaiiiiiiiiiihhhhou?

Let me out of here!
Aaaaauuuuuuuuuuuummmoooonnnnnn iiiiiiiii!

(Note: Accents vary from whale to whale. If you are speaking to a humpback, try to sound as if you have a terrible stomach ache. If you are talking to a blue whale, groan as if a walrus is sitting on your head.)

CHAPTER 8
DON'T FORGET TO LAUGH
EVERYONE LOVES A CLOWN(FISH)

It's a common misconception that clownfish are funny. Strictly speaking, clownfish are no funnier than any other type of fish. But it never hurts to have a few good jokes on hand for emergencies. Here are some of my favorites:

WHICH FISH WORK IN HOSPITALS?
Sturgeons!

WHERE DO FISH SLEEP?
On a water bed.

WHY ARE FISH SO SMART?
Because they live in schools.

WHAT DO YOU CALL A FISH WITH NO EYES?
A fsh.

WHICH FISH COSTS THE MOST?
A goldfish.

HOW DO YOU PAY FOR IT?
With sand dollars.

WHICH FISH MAKES THE TASTIEST SANDWICH?
A peanut butter and jellyfish.

WHAT KIND OF FISH LIVE IN HOLLYWOOD?
Starfish!

WHICH FISH HAVE THE MOST POWER?
Electric eels.

WHICH FISH WON THE BOAT RACE?
The sailfish!

WHY WAS THE WHALE CRYING?
Because he was a blue whale.

WHY WAS THE MUSSEL MAD AT THE CLAM?
Because he was being a little shellfish.

WHY DID THE TUNA CROSS THE ROAD?
To get to the other tide.

HOW DID THE TWO OCTOPUSES GO ON A DATE?
Hand in hand in hand in hand in hand in hand in hand in hand.

WHAT WAS THE NAME OF THE BLOWFISH WHO BECAME A RAP STAR?

Puff Daddy.

WHAT DOES A TROUT BECOME WHEN HE GOES TO HEAVEN?

An angelfish.

KNOCK, KNOCK.

Who's there?
Whale.
Whale who?
Whale you please let me in?
It's cold out here.

WHAT DID THE SHRIMP DETECTIVE SAY WHEN HE ARRIVED AT THE CRIME SCENE?

Something's fishy.

WHY DID THE CLOWNFISH LEAVE HOME?

He wanted to be with friends, not anemones.

KNOCK, KNOCK.

Who's there?

Fin.

Fin who?

Finish up this darn joke—
it's taking forever!

WHAT KIND OF FISH NEVER TELLS THE TRUTH?

A lionfish.

WHAT DO FISH LIKE TO DO AT A FOOTBALL GAME?

The wave.

IN CONCLUSION

So, now that you've read the book, I hope you're ready to get extreme. That's right—*extreme*-ly safe! Oh, I know it doesn't sound as exciting as shark-baiting or eel-boarding, or whatever it is you kids like to do these days, but believe me, a safe fish is a happy fish.

That said, also remember that there will be times in your life that are frightening or dangerous. When that happens, try to stay calm . . . and ask others for help. I know I never could have made it across the ocean without a little help from my friends.

My final piece of advice is to always believe in yourself. Even when things are scary, the one person you can always count on is you. Just keep your fins to the waves and keep on swimming.